Look and Find

Disney · PIXAR
ONWARD

we make books come alive®
pi kids
Phoenix International Publications, Inc.
Chicago • London • New York • Hamburg • Mexico City • Sydney

In times of old, the realm was a place of powerful magic, perilous quests, and fearless adventurers! But that was a long time ago. These days, Ian Lightfoot's greatest trial is avoiding awkward small talk with his New Mushroomton neighbors as he walks home from school.

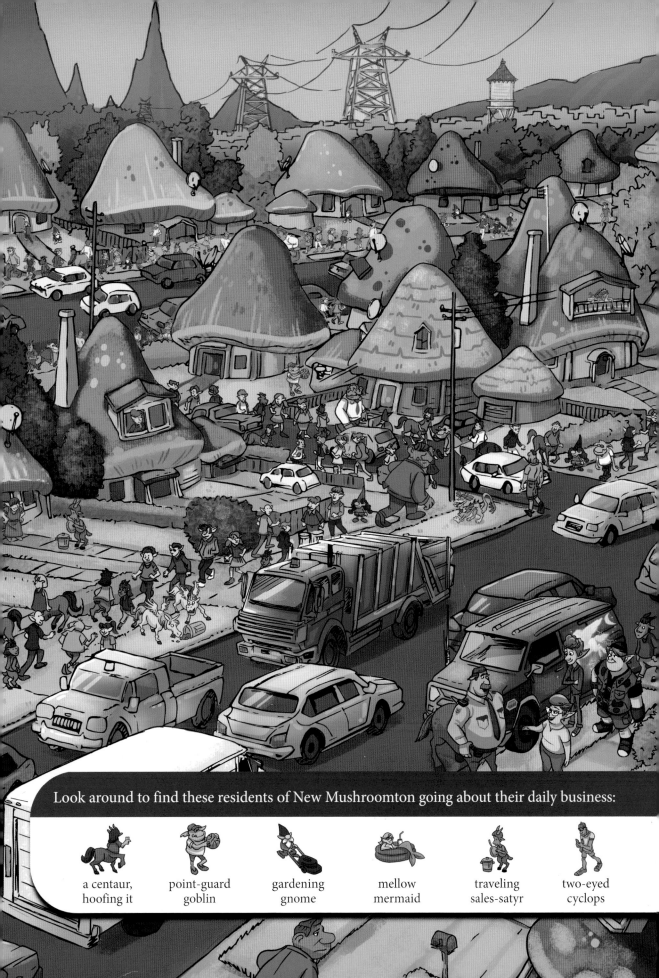

Look around to find these residents of New Mushroomton going about their daily business:

a centaur, hoofing it   point-guard goblin   gardening gnome   mellow mermaid   traveling sales-satyr   two-eyed cyclops

Happy sixteenth birthday, Ian! All he expects is a piece of cake, but instead, Ian and his brother Barley get an ancient magical staff and a message from their father, who died before Ian was born. The spell was supposed to bring their dad back for one day, but it doesn't go exactly as planned. Barley doesn't remember much about Dad, but he definitely remembers him having a top half!

Cast your eyes around Ian's room to find these things caught up in the magic spell:

Dad's
sweatshirt

special
cassette tape

Ian's
broken phone

this family
photo

this unfinished
homework

yesterday's
snack

To finish the spell, Ian and Barley must find a Phoenix Gem. They start where all quests begin: the Manticore's Tavern. But the Manticore is no longer the fearsome beast that she once was, and now her tavern is more about burgers and fries than adventures and quests. If Ian and Barley want a map to the Phoenix Gem, they'll have to use the one on the kids' menu.

Find your way through kids and servers and trays of food to spot these "authentic" tavern items:

the "magic" gift

"fair" fortune

fearless "Manticore"

griffin nuggets with fries

"official" quest map

"ancient" sword

Every quest needs a trusty steed! And no steed is trustier—or rustier—than Guinevere, Barley's van. Ian and Barley will be talking to Dad in no time, especially with Barley's historically accurate role-playing game, Quests of Yore, to guide them. All they need to do is follow the map, find the Phoenix Gem, finish the spell, and then make a lifetime's worth of memories with Dad before the sun sets tomorrow! Easy, right?

Buckle up and find these things in Barley's van:

dwindling provisions | van "repair" kit | tiny warrior | quest fuel | overdue library book | historically accurate questing guide

Only a few miles into the adventure, Guinevere sputters to a stop. She's out of gas! Ian tries to refill the tank with magic, but it backfires and suddenly his brother is pocket-sized! At the gas station, little Barley gets on the wrong side of the Pixie Dusters, a rough-riding group of sprites who don't appreciate Barley's helpful advice, or Dad's blank stare.

Browse the store to pick out these gas station goods:

Dragon Fancy
Magazine

Kracken
Kracklins

Energy Potion

Gorgonzola's
cheese puffs

Sparkle
Sticks

Dragon
Eggs

Ian and Barley's mom, Laurel, has teamed up with the Manticore to protect the boys on their quest. For that, Laurel needs Curse Crusher, the Manticore's ancient sword. But the Manticore ran into some tough times a few years ago, so she needs to make a quick stop at the Pawn Shop to buy back the only sword of its kind in all the land.

One creature's trash is this goblin's treasure! Take a look around Grecklin's shop to find these valuables:

rockin' record

garlic crusher

tasteful necklace

you don't want to know

almost-new TV

stylish helmet

After a treacherous trip down the Path of Peril, and a heart-pounding journey through an underground gauntlet, Ian and Barley finally arrive…back in New Mushroomton? But what about the Phoenix Gem? The sun is already setting! Ian thinks it's hopeless, but Barley listens to his gut. And his gut says that the Phoenix Gem must be around here somewhere.

After all of their adventures, the brothers find New Mushroomton a bit ordinary.
Look around for these dull, everyday things:

boring bench

standard
shopping bag

uninteresting
unicorn

cautious cone

ordinary
license plate

familiar flowers

Desperate for clues, Barley climbs into the fountain in the park. And…there is the Phoenix Gem! When he pulls the gem out of the fountain, red smoke billows out and turns the high school into a fire-breathing dragon! With the help of Mom, the Manticore, and his magic staff, Ian defeats the dragon—and the curse. The sun is about to set, but there are still a few precious minutes to spend with Dad.

Stay out of the way of the dragon as you search for these high-school things:

bullhorn

well-balanced meal

almost-A

regional champions' trophy

teacher's treat

torn-up textbook

Here, there be dragons! Go back to the New Mushroomton
suburbs to find these magical pets and creatures:

Don't get lost in the shuffle! Flip back to Ian's bedroom
to collect these Quests of Yore cards:

Cleanup at table three! Turn back to the Manticore's Tavern
and clear away these messes:

No parking! Drive back
to Barley's van and
find **10** parking tickets
that need to be paid.

Who you calling whimsical? Go back to the gas station
and find these sprites:

Mom and the Manticore are stuck in a sticky situation!
Turn back to Grecklin's Pawn Shop to find these spiderwebs:

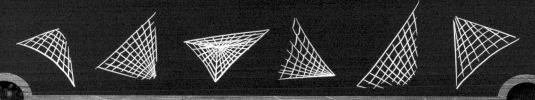

These are not the signs you're looking for. As Barley looks for a sign
from the universe, go back to downtown New Mushroomton to find these
more commonplace signs:

This is not a drill! Quickly and calmly turn back to the high school
dragon and find these things on fire:

Ian learns to be bold, just like
his dad, who wore purple socks
every single day. Look back
on Ian's journey and find
a purple sock hidden in
every scene.